HOT WHEELS

Cave Race!

By Ace Landers
Illustrated by Dave White

SCHOLASTIC INC.

New York   Toronto   London   Auckland

Sydney   Mexico City   New Delhi   Hong Kong

ISBN 978-0-545-20871-0

12 11 10 9 8 7 6 5 4   10 11 12 13 14 15/0

Printed in the U.S.A.   40
First printing, March 2010

The drivers are ready.
Where will the cars race today?

The race is in a cave!

START!

FINISH!

First, the cars speed downhill.

The cars turn on their headlights.

There is a hole ahead.

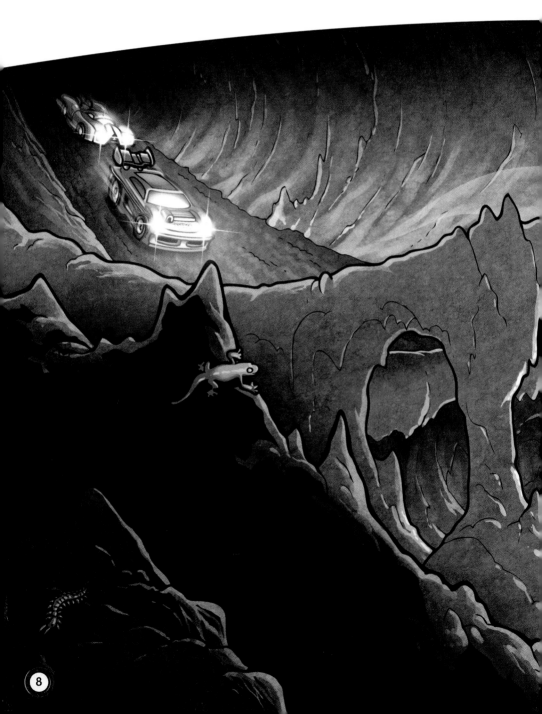

The first car lands safely!
The race goes deeper.

Caves have stalagmites on the ground.

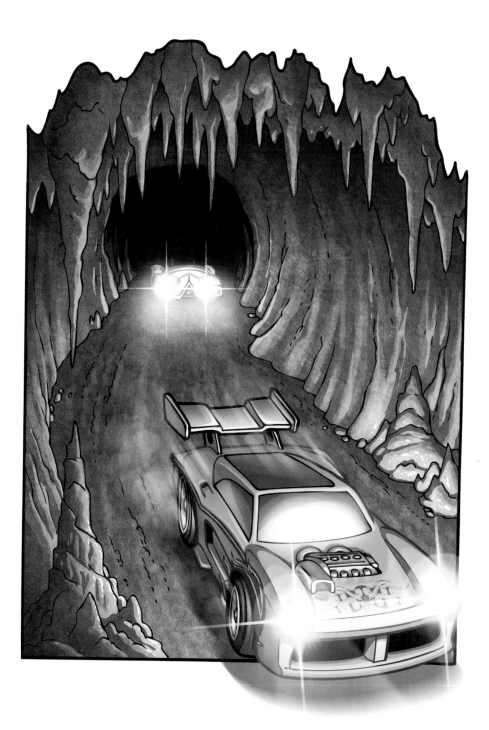

The stalagmites are sharp!

The green car hits a jump.

The green car takes the lead!

But the others are fast, too.

The cars zoom down
deeper into the cave.

The cars are too powerful for the cave.

The cave walls rumble and shake.

The purple car cannot stop in time!

What is that light in the distance?

21

There is a hole in the roof of the cave!

The cars race past the crowd.

The red car skids.
Watch out!
There is water on the track!

Something is glowing up ahead.

It is an underground lake!

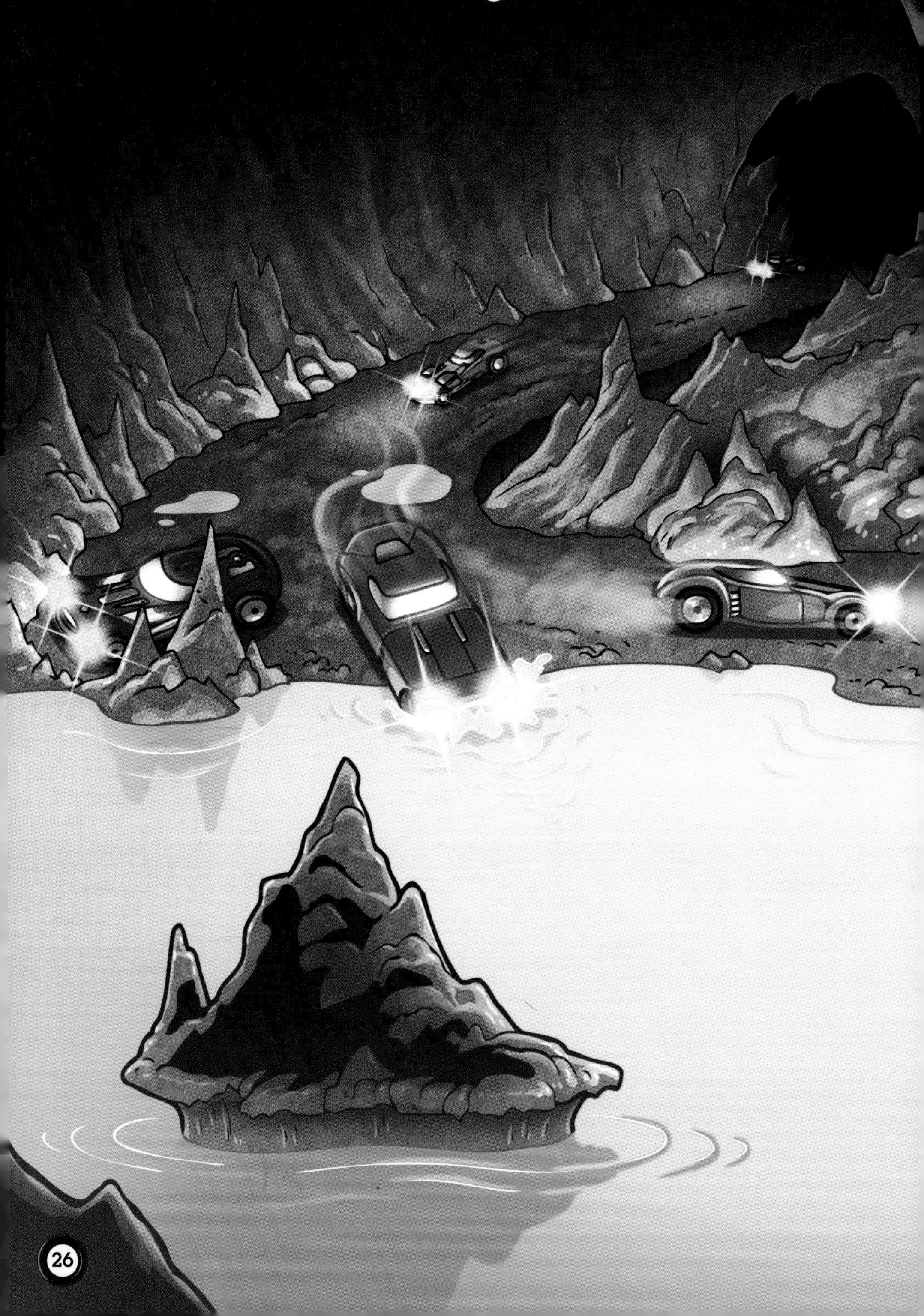

The cars swerve.
No one wants to go for a swim!

The green car is still winning.
Look! There is the finish line!

Wait!
What is that flapping sound?

Bats!

The green car cannot see the finish line!
The orange car is close.

The orange car wins!

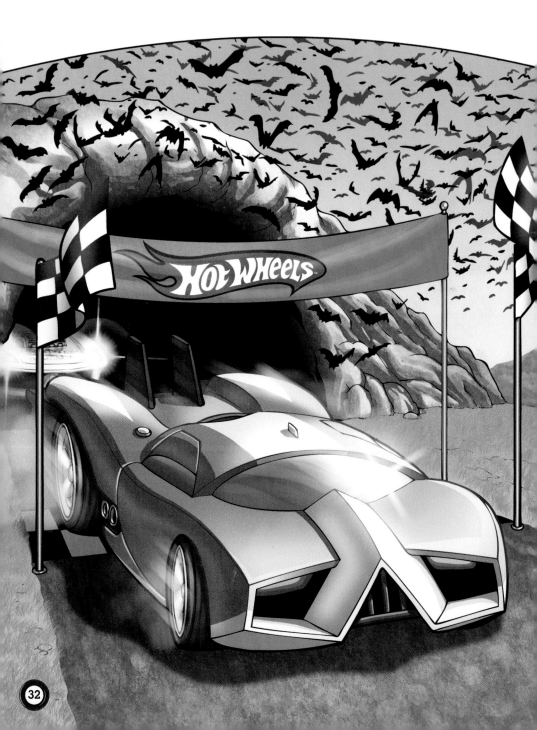